Illumen
Spring 2025

Edited by
Tyree Campbell

Illumen
Spring 2025

Edited by Tyree Campbell

Cover art "Woman with Wolf" by Richard E. Schell
Cover design by Laura Givens

Vol. XXII, No. 2   Spring 2025
Illumen [ISSN: 1558-9714] is published quarterly on the 1st days of January, April, July, and October in the United States of America by Hiraeth Publishing, P.O. Box 1248, Tularosa, NM 88352. Copyright 2025 by Hiraeth Publishing. All rights revert to authors and artists upon publication except as noted in selected individual contracts. Nothing may be reproduced in whole or in part without written permission from the authors and artists. Any similarity between places and persons mentioned in the fiction or semi-fiction and real places or persons living or dead is coincidental. Writers and artists guidelines are available online at www.albanlake.com/guidelines. Guidelines are also available upon request from Hiraeth Publishing, P.O. Box 1248, Tularosa, NM 88352, if request is accompanied by a SASE #10 envelope with a 60-cent US stamp. Editor: Tyree Campbell. Subscriptions: $28 for one year [4 issues], $54 for two years [8 issues]. Single copies $10.00 postage paid in the United States. Subscriptions to Canada: $32 for one year, $54 for two years. Single copies $12.00 postage paid to Canada. U.S. and Canadian subscribers remit in U.S. funds. All other countries inquire about rates.

New from Terrie Leigh Relf!!
Postcards From Space

Terrie Leigh Relf loves sending and receiving postcards from the four corners of the universe—and beyond! Postcards tell a story. They are mementos from friends and family—and from total strangers—and provide a glimpse into life's journeys, observations, and adventures.

Here are some messages on postcards from space, found aboard a derelict craft that crashed on an arid, lifeless world. The OSPS (Outer Space Postal Service) has delivered these messages to Terrie, who now presents them to you. This is what it is like out there.

https://www.hiraethsffh.com/product-page/postcards-from-space-by-terrie-leigh-relf

A Little Help, Please

In the world of the small indie press we fight a never-ending battle for attention to our work, as writers and in publishing. Here's an example: big publishers [you know who they are] have gobs of $$$ that they can devote to advertising and marketing. Here at Hiraeth Publishing, our advertising budget consists of the deposits for whatever soda bottles and aluminum cans we can find alongside the highways. Anti-littering laws make our task even more difficult . . . ☺

That's where YOU come in. YOU are our best promoter. YOU are the one who can tell others about us. Just send 'em to our website, tell them about our store. That's all. Just that.

Of course, we don't mind if you talk us up. We're pretty good, you know. We have some award-winning and award-nominated writers and artists, plus other voices well-deserving to be heard [not everyone wins awards, right?] but our publications are read-worthy nevertheless.

That number once again is:

www.hiraethsffh.com

Friend us on Facebook at Hiraeth Publish and follow us on Twitter at

@HiraethPublish1

Contents

Features
24	Featured Poet: Meg Smith
30	Book Review: Minimalism by Lisa Timpf

Poems
10	Exit Sandman by Alan Ira Gordon
14	Prayer to the Caladrius Bird by Claire Smith
15	Sunless by Oliver Smith
	Tanka by Alan Ira Gordon
16	The Insomniac by Stephanie Smith
18	Flying the Flag by John Grey
19	Once in a Blue Moon by Sandy Raschke
22	Devotional by Christine Blinn
23	Jupiter by Dennis Owen Frohlich
27	Green Hail by Denny Marshall
28	Four Monsters by Denise Noe
29	Ants & Aliens by Denny Marshall
34	Settlement on Org by John Grey
36	Cemetery Statue by Sterling Osborne
37	Once in a Blue Moon by Sandy Raschke
39	Derelict Hearts by Oliver Smith
40	My Oread's Voice by Sterling Osborne
41	The Astronaut Widow to Her Son by John Grey
42	To Steal by Claire Smith
43	The Watchers by Stephanie Smith
44	Speculations of Mystic Studies by John Wise

Illustrations
20	Ode to Chagall by Sandy DeLuca
38	Mushroom Dreams by Sandy DeLuca

SUBSCRIBE TO ILLUMEN!!

We'll be glad you did...
So will you.
Here's the link:

https://www.hiraethsffh.com/product-page/illumen-1

Support the small independent press!

You're not afraid of a little poetry, are you?

The Miseducation of the Androids
By William Landis

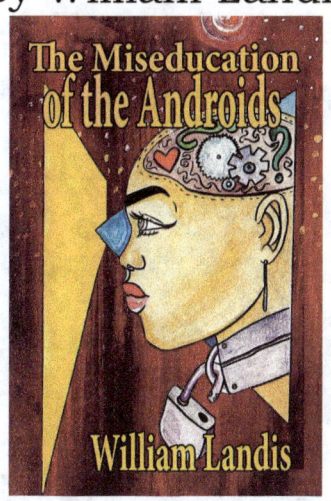

What happens when androids confront concepts inconsistent with their programming? William Landis examines this question by means of flash fiction and haiku that you will find pithy, poignant, and amusing.

William Landis is a science fiction poet from North Carolina. He is a graduate of North Carolina A&T State University, completing both undergraduate, and graduate work in agriculture. He is currently working on a vermicomposting project, and he is an Army reserve engineer officer. He enjoys running, writing, reading, and exploring new places.

Order a copy here: https://www.hiraethsffh.com/product-page/miseducation-of-the-androids-by-william-landis

Midnight Comes Early

By Marcie Lynn Tentchoff

Marcie Lynn Tentchoff lives on the west coast of Canada, in a forest of brambles and evergreens far too densely tangled to form the setting for any but the darkest of fairy tales. She writes poetry and stories that tiptoe worriedly along the border of speculation and horror, and is an active member of both the Science Fiction & Fantasy Poetry Association and the Horror Writers Association. Marcie is an Aurora Award winner, and her work has been either nominated, short, or long-listed for Stoker, Rhysling, and British Fantasy awards. She is very much involved in middle grade and YA media, and edits Spaceports & Spidersilk, a magazine aimed at readers from 8-9 up to (and past!) 89. When she is not involved with the practice of placing and editing words on a page, she teaches creative writing and acting for a performing arts studio.

Order a copy here...

https://www.hiraethsffh.com/product-page/midnight-comes-early-by-marcie-lynn-tentchoff

Exit Sandman
Alan Ira Gordon

I can't tell you how long
I've been at it. Sprinkling my dust
into young eyes to hasten sweet
dreaming. I can say that it's been
long enough and time now for
a successor.

But here's the thing: these days,
it isn't working. Oh, I still make
the nighttime rounds and do my duty.
But the result is nothing/nada/nyet.
The younglings sleep but perchance
don't dream. I don't need the proof
of why. I feel the answer in my heart
and bones.

It's the internet's fault. The short
attention-span theatre of Instagram/
Snapchat/Tik-Tok/Pinterest. And
of course the Twitter.

Cybernetic seedlings metastasizing
throughout the all-consciousness.
Thinning the surface of reason.
Scarring thought. Dreamkillers all.
Impervious to my power.

My predecessor recruited me the old-
fashioned way, a simple newspaper
ad piquing my interest. Updating
with the times, I planned on placing
a Monster.com or LinkedIn notice.

But feeling this evening's completion,
the world-wide fruition of newfound
dreamless void? What's the use.
Like the Age of Magic before us,
perhaps the Age of Dreams has
also passed.

So tonight. For the first time ever.
The Sandman won't make his rounds
amongst humanity's young. I'll sit
it out and see if I'm missed by
anyone at all.

Most likely not, as in the darkness
I'll wait and see. But perhaps.
I hope so. I pray.

I can dream,
can't I?

Pittsburgh
and Other Poems
By Alan Ira Gordon

Pittsburgh and Other Poems

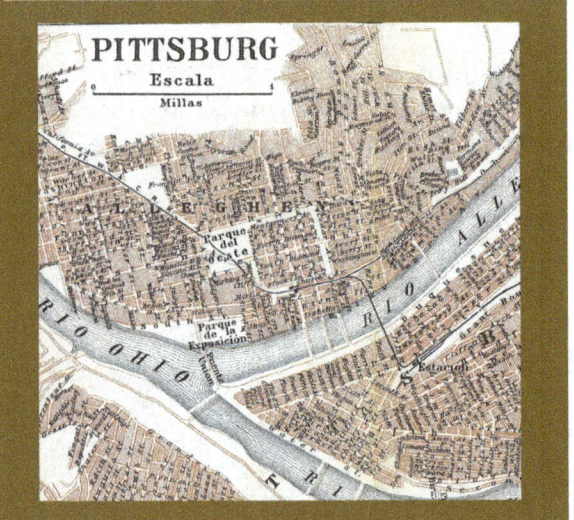

Alan Ira Gordon

Sometimes a sense of place is easy to identify and understand. In those instances, it can be a physical city, town, neighborhood or just a piece of property. Other times it can be a point in time, either past, present or future. And in yet other instances it can be a more exotic or alien sense of place, perhaps intergalactic, or multi-universe, even an alternate reality version of a well-known place and time, existing at a quantum point or merely within the minds of writers and readers.

All of the poems in this book explore in poetic form various ideas of sense of place, whether physical locations, points in time or ideas of place that could only exist (for now, at least) within the creative realms of science fiction, fantasy and/or horror.

Print: https://www.hiraethsffh.com/product-page/pittsburgh-other-poems-by-alan-ira-gordon

ePub: https://www.hiraethsffh.com/product-page/pittsburgh-other-poems-by-alan-ira-gordon-2

PDF: https://www.hiraethsffh.com/product-page/pittsburgh-other-poems-by-alan-ira-gordon-1

Prayer to the Caladrius Bird
Claire Smith

During the night when the lamp was lit darkness came upon the room. Smoke rose up from the floor and in the smoke was a pigeon with white borders*

Turn your head, just once, do not stare straight
into my eyes. You're here at midnight
regular as the clock's strike. At ten they turn

down the strip-lights in the corridor outside,
my room is lit by a solitary lamp. Smoke swirls
wingtips unfurl from under the bed; a spectre,

your breast swells, you glide across the ceiling.
Your plumage radiates pearls, your eyes glint
amber. One more night let your feathers brush

against my face; raise up in smoke-whisps. Grant
my wish to lay myself out forever and ever,
                              in a
                  permanent sleep.

*Gloucester, Gloucestershire Archives (GA), Item Reference HO22. 83/2/63, accession number 15507 (Bundle), Mary Agg (Housewife), Facts indicating insanity observed by myself, Medical Certificate (No. 1168), signed by Robert Kirklands, (Batchelor of Medicine and Master of Surgery of Glasgow University), County and City of Gloucester Pauper Lunatic Asylum, in Wotton near Gloucester, 6th / 7th November 1883.

Sunless
Oliver Smith

A planet in the void where comets secreted
life in cold atmosphere driven by lightning's flash;
life that never saw a bright sun's beating heart
just a lesser cold in its photons' greyish wash;
life grown like crystals from primordial frost
in orbits spun on the wheel of distant gravity
so far from fire: a world of iron, ice, and rock.
From another place, powered by atoms' decay,
the rocket descended burning stronger by far
than any flame seen here before; its payload
carried beyond the shockwave of the star
to examine the thing frost and darkness brewed.
Out bound from night-lands slow towards the ship
impatient for new worlds: greedy, life creeps.

Confusion reigns as alien visitors
unable to differentiate between
humans and our doggo companions;
from extraterrestrial viewpoint,
we simply all look alike.

~Alan Ira Gordon

The Insomniac
Stephanie Smith

She lies in bed, dodging stars she thinks
    are nightmares
sent down from the heavens to tear her apart

She feels trapped in a cold, dark place where
not even moonlight can save her

It's as if she's burned off her eyelids to stay awake.
Shadows grab her. The hours drag

She floats in a limbo between flesh and death
where sleep is just a memory,

a fairy tale or lullaby like a dirge song
luring her to the grave

The newest from G. O. Clark!!!
Mindscapes

G. O. Clark takes on the future in this riveting collection of poetic observations about life, the Universe, and everything else. He takes you up mountains and down valleys, and always makes you wonder about what's happening and what will happen (if we aren't careful).

Ordering links:
Print: https://www.hiraethsffh.com/product-page/mindscapes-by-g-o-clark
ePub: https://www.hiraethsffh.com/product-page/mindscapes-by-g-o-clark-2
PDF: https://www.hiraethsffh.com/product-page/mindscapes-by-g-o-clark-1

Flying The Flag
John Grey

Another planet in the name of my countrymen –
yes, this is the place.

Plant the flag in a bare patch of ground
without a thought to time lost, money spent,
and a dozen serious cases of home-sickness
and head-worm.

And yet, they call us
the guardians of all dreams.

Some, on Earth,
would even mistake this dead place for a cradle.

Cradle of what?
Not civilization?
Maybe the cradle of a solitary flag?

Yes, Earth,
billions of people
banging on the bars of their cages,
still believing that something wonderful
awaits them on the other side.

It is midnight, prisoner's time.

Here, it's Flag Day.
But only if we make it back to the ship.
Only if, we take one glance back
and, for the last time,
see the future flying.

Once in a Blue Moon
Sandy Raschke

Her eyes, cold,
and hard as sapphires

blood coursing,
she grips the spear,
veins knotting;
below the blue moon
the deep sea roils
black as coal,
the waves, indigo,
glimmering in its wake;
the huntress stalks,
creature of the night;
the starship lifts,
eyes dimming, dying,

her heart, cold,
    quickening like the prey.

Ode to Chagall by Sandy DeLuca

The Mayfly Moons
By Shawn Vimislicky

Fantasy poetry at its finest, with new observations on classical literature, self-discovery, the longing for a better place (hiraeth), beings swept up in events, and fantasy romanticism. Often uplifting, sometimes darker, and here and there a mix of the two extremes, this collection will thrill you, haunt you, and raise your spirits.

Print: https://www.hiraethsffh.com/product-page/mayfly-moons-by-shawn-vimislicky-2
PDF: https://www.hiraethsffh.com/product-page/mayfly-moons-by-shawn-vimislicky-1
ePub: https://www.hiraethsffh.com/product-page/mayfly-moons-by-shawn-vimislicky

Look up at the stars you say, while the porch swing rocks and sways

As if the inky black sky could teleport us into an interstellar getaway

The stars we wished on each and every night would twinkle and swirl as we sped by out of sight

To a galaxy not so far away where we could lay beneath the ruins of some past primitive life

Sharing our devotions each and every night, and when we tired of the

Relentless pull of the moon we would take off to another realm

Where the Milky Way is our ocean, and watch cosmic waves in motion

Washing up twinkling stars on the shore at our feet, and as you gaze

Down into my eyes brushing the stardust off my cheek

I know no matter what planet we are on

You will always make me weak

~Christine Blinn

Jupiter
Dennis Owen Frohlich

Swirling bands of clouds, azure, gold, and green
spiraling whorls of color, tan and tangerine
Metallic hydrogen seas are churning,
blue aurorae tingling, burning
The king of planets ever shines
upon the children of the earth

Rings on rings, however faint
steadfast gravity shows no restraint,
countless moons Zeus has accrued
From the makeshift lens were viewed
by a man who reads the signs
of Jupiter's surpassing worth

Galileo uncovered the secret math
and so incurred the church's wrath
They sentenced him to house arrest,
thinking this would end his quest
But knowledge cannot be confined
after imagination gives birth

Featured Poet: Meg Smith

The Martian Tide

My fingers ran long rows,
irrigated with tears
in the rust of sand.
Such was our shore.
But it drew in, and drew out,
only snarls of cold air,
sending up spirals of scarlet
dust, falling, collapsing
under their own frozen
sense without ice, or ice crystals.
Such would require water,
and we had already sent our prayers
north, and south, to unyielding poles.
A blue world hovers, ridiculous,
on one horizon.
A plume of raging storms,
 froth of another world,
rises, holding court among
its own world nursery.
Tired, I grew, raising my own hand
to the pale sun of indifference,
a prayer answered only
with a shadow of long streaks.

Woman of the Blood Sky

Her name appears
as if in an offering
in a garland of roses;
she does not speak it,
but knows it, mutely.
Her one true voice carries lightning,
a journeywork of dust, fire, and
a fissure in the black dome.
Through the light, she bleeds.
The flowers will raise their heads,
unbowed, and will grow deep,
crimson, and strong.

Darkness Canticle

If you sing to me
your demon song,
I will exhale it in dust,
and the night will dissolve it.
The air chills, and grasps all.
Songs and bodies
become nothing.
Light finds only bare traces,
drawn in scrolls
along a shifting earth.
That's all that withers,
all that speaks
the music of our fading, forever.

World of Hithering

Dawn calls
with diamonds
in a shimmering blear
along treetops.
The waking is false:
the copper streak falls,
a sun not yet born,
a planet not yet old.
Ridiculous, and yet we remain
hungry, unsleeping,
until we become like frost
unrelenting.

Meg Smith is a writer, journalist, dancer and events producer living in Lowell, Mass.

In addition to previously appearing in *Illumen*, her poetry and fiction has appeared in *The Horror Zine, Raven Cage, Strange Horizons, Silver Blade, The Cafe Review, Muddy River Poetry Review, Sirens Call, Dark Dossier, Dark Moon Digest,* and many more.

She is the creator of Poe in Lowell, a festival honoring Edgar Allan Poe's three visits to Lowell.

She is author of six poetry books and a short fiction collection, *The Plague Confessor*. She welcomes visits to megsmithwriter.com.

Green Hail
Denny E. Marshall

Golf ball size green hail
Falls down on the ground
Without causing damage
Or making sound

Drops sprout arms and legs
Then uncover face
Tiny aliens have
Arrived from space

Thousands of them
Eating insects and weeds
Also variety
Of grass and seeds

Once group full
Quickly return to the sky
They mean no harm
Just like to eat and fly

Four Monsters
Denise Noe

Frankenstein, robot, or mummy,
a monster is a cumbersome thing
You would escape the laggard, easily,
if you just kept on running
but running at a good speed, without
stumbling and without looking back
at mummy, Frankenstein, or robot:
cloddish, slow-moving maniac.

What would you expect?
Frankenstein: a single unit from dead rabble,
Neurotransmitters firing cues
to a fleshly Tower of Babel.
The robot was designed with great care
and painstakingly constructed,
but the programming was flawed,
leaving the poor robot rattle-pated.

The mummy awakened from a dreamless sleep,
by his linens confined,
He thinks, "This cannot be Paradise"
a reward would not leave him blind!
Why were you afraid? For robot,
Frankenstein, or mummy, were lost:
Foreigners without a home country,
into your land abruptly tossed.

They approached you, at a painful toddle,
wanting to ask directions.

You ran, heart pounding and sweat burning,
though they waved neither knives nor guns.
Ow!--your face *smacked* a tree.
When the ensuing shock broke your heart's lifeline,
You were felled by a monster called fear,
not robot, mummy, or Frankenstein.

Ants & Aliens
Denny E. Marshall

Aliens visit an anthill
Since they're about the same size
Communicate freely
By touching antennas
Help them build and gather food
Pay homage to their queen
Flood them with light
Of I.Q. extender
Show them how
To build tiny weapons
Not long after
No human trespasses

Minimalism: A Handbook of Minimalist Genre Poetic Forms, edited by Teri Santitoro
Reviewed by Lisa Timpf

Minimalism: A Handbook of Minimalist Genre Poetic Forms, edited by Teri Santitoro, is a helpful compendium of over forty speculative poetry forms. Some, such as scifaiku, sci(na)ku, haibun, and fibonacci, will be familiar to practitioners of speculative minimalist poetry. The handbook also includes less frequently seen forms like acrostiku, empat perkataan, and fortune cookie poems.

Chapters are written by a number of speculative poetry writers, including Herb Kauderer, David C. Kopaska-Merkel, Joshua Gage, Robert E. Porter, and Marge Simon, to name a few. Generally, each chapter offers an explanation of the form, sometimes including its historic origin. Many of the authors, like Joshua Gage in his article on horror ku, go beyond the nuts-and-bolts and provide guidance regarding the nuances of the form. Usually, at least one example of the form, and sometimes several, are offered. Some chapters also conclude with references or suggestions for further reading.

A few forms have more than one chapter devoted to them, providing multiple perspectives on how to craft that variety of poem. The section on scifaiku, for example, offers perspectives from Joshua Gage, Jean-Paul Garnier, Francis W. Alexander, and Wendy Van Camp. The variety in authors also provides for a variety of tones. Some articles are serious, while Robert E. Porter's take on horror ku, as an example, is playful as well as informative.

Though a number of the articles are reprinted from *Scifaikuest* poetry magazine, others were written specifically for the handbook. Chapter length varies from topic to topic. Some entries, like the ones on acrostiku and Australian couplets, are one-pagers, while SciFaiKasen and empat perkataan each have seven pages allotted to them. The book is arranged with the poetic forms in alphabetical order, facilitating its use as a quick reference.

Reading *Minimalism: A Handbook of Minimalist Genre Poetic Forms* encouraged me to try forms I hadn't experimented with previously, such as dragonfly fibonaccis, cherita, fortune cookie poems, and even a Simon sijo. The book earned its keep by inspiring new poems that were subsequently sold.

I found it helpful to read *Minimalism: A Handbook of Minimalist Genre Poetic Forms* from cover to cover first, acquainting myself with the contents. Some of the forms seemed to be begging for a trial, so I started by working with those. During National Poetry Month, on days when the daily prompts didn't particularly appeal to me, I turned to *Minimalism* for inspiration.

Just over 200 pages in length, *Minimalism: A Handbook of Minimalist Genre Poetic Forms* offers a useful reference for both aspiring and experienced writers of minimalist genre poetry.

Minimalism:

A Handbook of Minimalist Genre Poetic Forms

This handbook contains articles about how to write various minimalist poetry forms such as scifaiku, senryu, sijo, haibun, empat perkataan, ghazals, cinquain, cherita, rengays, rengu, octains, tanka, threesomes, and many more. Each article is written by an expert in that particular poetry form.

Teri Santitoro, aka sakyu, who assembled this handbook, has been the editor of Scifaikuest since 2003.

https://www.hiraethsffh.com/product-page/minimalism-a-handbook-of-minimalist-genre-poetic-forms

Settlement On Org
John Grey

On Org, the fires are incessant.
It's as if everything
on the planet is flammable.
Not just the foliage, the settlements, .
the minerals in the soil,
but the very hot air we breathe.
This world is its own arsonist.
It doesn't need an electrical fault
or a lightning strike.

And yet, this land we strive to conquer
is a master of regeneration.
With conflagration,
it razes what it finds no long useful,
supplants it with all that is new and fertile.

But we're human.
To us, the flames are all about death.
Yet nothing is truly lost.
Even our ashes feed into the cycles.
Like it or not.
every blade of fresh grass,
each developing tree root,
contains a little
of those who have gone before.

Org can surprise you.
Despite its ruthlessness,
it knows how to fashion a beautiful,
if temporary, landscape.
And not just beautiful.
Familiar also.

The Future Adventures of Bailey Belvedere

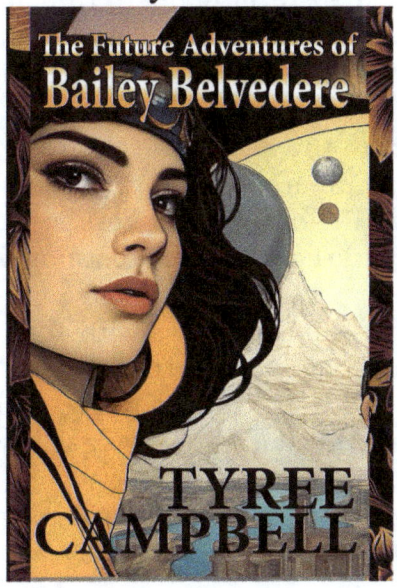

https://www.hiraethsffh.com/product-page/further-adventures-of-bailey-belvedere-by-tyree-campbell

Cemetery Statue
Sterling Osborne

She holds a lantern out for men who died
in Christ. She keeps it lit beneath the moon
and when the rain and thunder dare to hide
the sun. Her smile at midnight and at noon

brings comfort to the keepers of the yard;
her hands of stone are loyal to their cause
and drive away the dark when work is hard
and dusk and starlight neither rest nor pause

to let the diggers fill the graves with soil.
She sees nobody walk the paths, and yet
her eyes are kind to those who grieve and toil.
When earth is heaved and heavy casket's set

beneath the ground, she holds the dark at bay
and guides the soul unto eternal day.

Once in a Blue Moon
Sandy Raschke

Her eyes, cold,
and hard as sapphires

blood coursing,
she grips the spear,
veins knotting;
below the blue moon
the deep sea roils
black as coal,
the waves, indigo,
glimmering in its wake;
the huntress stalks,
creature of the night;
the starship lifts,
eyes dimming, dying,

her heart, cold,
    quickening like the prey.

Mushroom Dreams
Sandy DeLuca

Derelict Hearts
Oliver Smith

They set you down by the stilled hearth.
Your home is all cracks and cellars,
where you might have lived had you
not been, every night, an empty skin;
pasted over walls like cheap paper
to conceal stains and rumors
of ruin that the cold north wind
whispered bitterly
through the broken windows.

Your music hides in-between bricks
and boards; behind unopened doors.
You revive your old bow but he
is rosin-thirsty and cannot
sing. Still you will try; try to coax
him to a waltz, but he is dry
and the dead-cat yowls, stretched
too-far, on the finger-board.
The tuning strays, it turns feral

and it shreds the notes that flutter
like broken moths; muted on wings
that glitter decay, verdigris, and rust.
The phrasing is frigid, as cold
as the two brass pennies you pressed
to sooth your tired eyes, grown red
in silence between the darkness
un-illuminated and emptiness,
unfilled.

You rock in the chair; you might be
a storm tossed boat, but ever dust
lies heavier, more is unmoved
every day. Four walls, a ceiling.
and a floor; nailed, each to the other,
make your room a hollow place like
an empty heart where an hourglass
that pumps the sand grain by grain
is upended again; one more time.

My Oread's Voice
Sterling Osborne

She sings to keep the thunder god in line
and calls his golden lightning drake to heel
and summons rain (when we both please to feel
each other's skin) to mute her moans and mine.
She works the earth with hymns to undermine
the devils lurking in our yard, to heal
our garden's clutching soil, to reveal
gardenias where there once was choking vine.
Though small, my oread's voice will command
the strongest of monochromatic spells
to bend the flight of arrows shot by hand
of fiend and beckon pails to draw from wells
the living stream which tongues of men demand
and which the oldest of her lyrics tells.

The Astronaut Widow To Her Son
John Grey

You see stars
where I know only ghosts.
You're dazzled
by lions and crabs and rams –
any creature that's not really there.
But I seek out the human dust,
the scattered particles,
the doomed of takeoff or reentry.
You make of constellations
what you will,
diagrams in the sky,
connected by your imagination.
I summon up
the moment before a ship exploded,
the moment after,
sense the brutal silence
that follows the adrenalin highs.
Your sky is a carnival of wonders.
Mine is a casket.

To Steal
Claire Smith

Steal
> *verb*
> 1. [...] *to take something from a person, shop, etc. without permission and without intending to return it or pay for it.*
> 2. *to move secretly and quietly so that other people do not notice you**

The boy thieved me from the ogre's shoe-rack
complete with my leather uppers,
snake laces and magic soles.

The boy snacked on juicy stars
as if they were wild blackberries
while stormy weather watered his thirst.

I took him hopping over mountains, striding
fast flowing rivers, treading from a forest's edge

to its clearing. All the time we widened our distance
from the ogre's anger, sneaked under his radar of
rage. We clouded his crystal ball's clarity.

I lengthened every step
      twenty-one miles distance
          between the boy and the ogre's netting,
              his carving knife,
              his frying-pan's spitting fat.

The Watchers
Stephanie Smith

They watch me from somewhere outside my dream
Somewhere along the edge of space
Like nameless faces in a worn-out place

They speak in whispers,
Carefully choosing their rhyme and meter,
What shade to paint the night

They linger in shadows,
Phasing in and out of dimensions,
Subsisting on strands of light

They pass through walls like memories
Daytime destroyed by false logic
A tired star gone supernova

Speculations of Mystic Studies
John Wise

I.

Blue-tinted windows capture the earliest fingers of sunlight. Dew-rich petals bow under the soft teeth of a gentle breeze. In whorls of color, faeries gather clandestine. The first blade of grass shrugs its shoulders, awake.

II.

Rain ricochets off the forest floor. Prances amid fungal huddles. Faerie rings. Sea-wind ponders the carved waters. Mermaid tails. Sleep shakes from petals' eyelashes. A brown recluse knits silver sunlight into worlds of dew. Drips from its silk-spun web.

III.

To look into the future, study puddles. Prismatic sheen of oils, unmixed. Gravel in your caruncles. Amphibian-wet. Fog rises, billows, reaches for the tops of trees. Fog dense and sculpted like marble.

>   A ribcage of feathers,
>   Songs thought lost
>   —Descendant's past

www.ingramcontent.com/pod-product-compliance
Lightning Source LLC
LaVergne TN
LVHW021953060526
838201LV00049B/1691